characters created by
lauren child

Snow
is my
FAVOURITE
and my best

PUFFIN

Charlie
and
Lola™

Text based on script written by Samantha Hill

Illustrations from the TV animation produced by Tiger Aspect

PUFFIN BOOKS
Published by the Penguin Group: London, New York, Australia,
Canada, India, Ireland, New Zealand and South Africa
Penguin Books Ltd, Registered Offices: 80 Strand, London WC2R 0RL, England

puffinbooks.com

First published 2006
This edition published 2008
1 3 5 7 9 10 8 6 4 2
Text and illustrations copyright © Lauren Child/Tiger Aspect Productions Limited, 2006
The Charlie and Lola logo is a trademark of Lauren Child
All rights reserved
The moral right of the author/illustrator has been asserted
Made and printed in China
ISBN: 978-1-856-13185-8

This edition produced for The Book People Ltd,
Hall Wood Avenue, Haydock, St Helens WA11 9UL

I have this little sister Lola.
    She is small and very funny.
Today Lola is extremely excited
    because the man on the weather
says it's going to snow.

Lola cannot wait for the snow to come.

She says, "Snow is my favourite

and is my best."

I say, "Remember, Lola,

snow can only come when it is very, very cold.

Dad said it might not snow until midnight.

Or even tomorrow."

"I know,"
        says Lola,
"but it is extremely
        cold right now.
So I think the
snow will come
sooner rather
        than midnight."

At bedtime, Lola says,
    "Do you think it has
started **snowing** now, Charlie?"

"No, go to sleep, Lola."

She says, "I can't because
    it might come while
I'm asleep, **sleeping**.

I'll just do **one more**
check...
        No snow.
    Not yet."

"See?" I say.
"Go to sleep."

But a little bit later
I hear Lola creeping
out of bed again.

"Ooooh!" she says.
"It's **Snowing!**
Charlie, come quick.
It's **Snowing**, it's really,
really Snowing!"

So I watch the snow with Lola.
She says, "Can we go out
and play in it now?"

"Not now, Lola," I say. "Wait until morning.
Then there'll be more and we can
go on the sledge with Marv and Sizzles.
And you can build a snowman if you want."

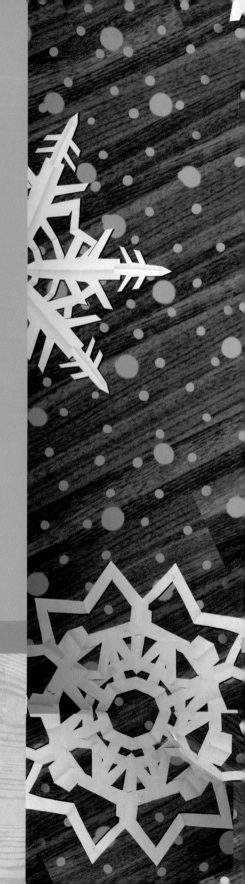

In the morning,
Lola shouts,

"Charlie!
Get up, Charlie!
Mum! Dad!

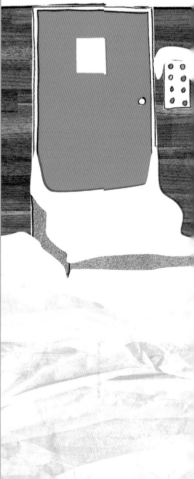

It's all gone
extremely white!"

So Mum and Dad took us to
the park and Lola was right,
everything had turned extremely,
completely white.

Then we see Marv and Lotta.
        And I say, "Where's Sizzles?"

"Yes," says Lola, "where's Sizzles?"

Marv points to a small pile of snow.
        "He's here!"
                he says. "Look!"

Lotta and Lola
make snow angels.

Lola says,
"Snow
is my
favourite
and my
best."

"I love **SnOw!**" says Lotta. "It's my **best** too."

Then we find a big hill and we all
go on the sledge. Even Sizzles!

I say, "Ready?
Steady?
Go!"

Wheeeeeeee

eeeeee!

Then me and Marv
build a **snowman**.

Lotta says,
"Let's make a
Snow doggy.
Come on, Lola!"

Later we go home to have some hot chocolate.
Marv says, "Mmmm. I love hot chocolate!"
Lola says,
"I love snow. Tomorrow I might put snowdog
and Sizzles on the sledge for a ride."

"I'm going to make a snow kennel," says Lotta,
"... and what about snow puppies?"

"Yes!" says Lola. "We can have lots of snow puppies!"

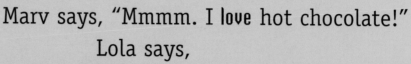

But when we go to the park the next day,
Lola can't make anything.

"It's **gone!**" she says.

"All the lovely **snow** is absolutely **gone**.
There's **no** more **white**, Charlie.
It's all **cold**
and **wet**
and **brown**.
And **snowdog's gone**."

So we go home again.

Lola says,
"Why can't we
have **snow**
every day?"

And I say,
"Because it wouldn't be special.
Imagine you had a birthday
every day, so you had parties
and cakes and presents
all the time."

And Lola says,
"What's wrong with having
birthdays every day?"

And I say,
"It wouldn't be a treat, would it? I'm not
sure you would like snow every day."

"I would, Charlie," says Lola.
"Snow is my favourite
and is my best."

Then I have a really good idea.
"Well, imagine a
completely white land...

... where it's snowy and cold every day.
It's called the Arctic."

"Look at the polar bear," says Lola.
"What's he doing, Charlie?"
I say, "He's going for a swim."

"I'd like to go swimming," says Lola.
"Where's the beach?"
I say,
"There isn't a beach, Lola.
It's far too cold for us to go swimming."

Then I say, "And then there's this place right at the very bottom of the world, called the Antarctic, where you get seals and whales and ...."

"Penguins!" says Lola.
"Don't the penguins look smart,
Charlie! They look like they're
going to a party!
I wish I was wearing my best, smartest
party dress, you know, the stripy one."

And I say,
"You couldn't wear your stripy dress in the Antarctic.
You have to wear your coat all the time
because it's so cold."

"Oh yes," says Lola, "I forgot."

Then I say, "But when it's all snowy, you can do this...

...says, "but can we go home now?"

And I say, "But why? I thought snow was your favourite and was your best!"

"Come on!"

And we slide on the ice with the penguins.

And I say, "Isn't it amazing?"

"Wow!" says Lola.

"Yes, Charlie," she

Lola says, "I do like it, Charlie. But I'm just a little chilly!"

"Snow is my favourite and my best, Charlie," says Lola, "but if it was snowy all the time there would be lots of things you couldn't do. So we're maybe lucky, we can do swimming and have stripy dresses and have snow.

But I do feel sad that the snow has all gone."

So I say, "I've got a

urprise for you.
Don't look round!"

"A teeny weeny snowman
who lives in the freezer!"
says Lola. "How did he
get in there?"

"I don't know!" I say.

Lola says, "He's **melting!**"
I say, "Shall I put him back
in the **freezer** so we can keep him?"
"Oh **no**, Charlie," says Lola.
"Let's watch him **melt!**"